92
THA

Faber, Doris

Margaret Thatcher,
Britain's "Iron
Lady"

$10.95   p

DATE			
SEP 2 1 '98			

About the WOMEN OF OUR TIME™ Series

Today more than ever, children need role models whose lives can give them the inspiration and guidance to cope with a changing world. *WOMEN OF OUR TIME*, a series of biographies focusing on the lives of twentieth-century women, is the first such series designed specifically for the 7–11 age group. International in scope, these biographies cover a wide range of personalities—from historical figures to today's headliners—in such diverse fields as politics, the arts and sciences, athletics, and entertainment. Outstanding authors and illustrators present their subjects in a vividly anecdotal style, emphasizing the childhood and youth of each woman. More than a history lesson, the *WOMEN OF OUR TIME* books offer carefully documented life stories that will inform, entertain, and inspire the young people of our time.

Also in the WOMEN OF OUR TIME Series

BABE DIDRIKSON: Athlete of the Century
by R. R. Knudson

BETTY FRIEDAN: A Voice for Women's Rights
by Milton Meltzer

DOROTHEA LANGE: Life Through the Camera
by Milton Meltzer

DOLLY PARTON: Country Goin' to Town
by Susan Saunders

ELEANOR ROOSEVELT: First Lady of the World
by Doris Faber

DIANA ROSS: Star Supreme
by James Haskins

MARGARET THATCHER

BRITAIN'S "IRON LADY"

BY DORIS FABER

Illustrated by Robert Masheris

VIKING KESTREL

VIKING KESTREL

Viking Penguin Inc., 40 West 23rd Street, New York, New York 10010, U.S.A.
Penguin Books Ltd, Harmondsworth, Middlesex, England
Penguin Books Australia Ltd, Ringwood, Victoria, Australia
Penguin Books Canada Limited, 2801 John Street, Markham, Ontario, Canada L3R 1B4
Penguin Books (N.Z.) Ltd, 182–190 Wairau Road, Auckland 10, New Zealand

First published in 1985 by Viking Penguin Inc.
Published simultaneously in Canada

"Women of Our Time" is a trademark of Viking Penguin Inc.

Library of Congress Cataloging in Publication Data
Faber, Doris,   Margaret Thatcher, Britain's "Iron Lady."
(Women of our time)
1. Thatcher, Margaret—Juvenile literature.   2. Prime ministers—Great Britain—
Biography—Juvenile literature.   I. Masheris, Robert.   II. Title.   III. Series.
DA591.T47F32   1985   941.085'7'0924 [B]   85-40442   ISBN 0-670-80785-0

Printed in the United States of America by
The Book Press, Brattleboro, Vermont
Set in Garamond #3
1   2   3   4   5   89   88   87   86   85

Library of Congress Cataloging in Publication Data
Faber, Doris.   Margaret Thatcher, Britain's "Iron Lady."

CONTENTS

MARGARET THATCHER
BRITAIN'S "IRON LADY"

1

Above the Shop

The great city of London surrounds us. A big red bus, two stories tall, comes rumbling along. We climb aboard and ride to the railroad station called King's Cross.

Soon our silver train is gliding through the tidy English countryside. Out of the windows we see green fields dotted with grazing sheep. Then, in an hour or so, a few small factories appear.

"GRAN-tham!" the conductor cries.

Here is our stop. We have traveled more than a hundred miles from busy, exciting London to this quiet old town—because it's in Grantham that the story of Margaret Thatcher begins.

Now the whole world knows Mrs. Thatcher as the first woman Prime Minister of Great Britain, and the first woman ever to head the government of a major country in Europe or America. "The Iron Lady," her enemies nicknamed her during the 1970s. "They were right," Mrs. Thatcher herself said. "Britain *needs* an Iron Lady."

But when she was growing up in Grantham, she was just a strong-minded girl named Margaret Roberts.

At the age of nine, she won a poetry-reading contest. "You were lucky, Margaret," the head of her school congratulated her.

Margaret shook her head. "I wasn't lucky," she said. "I deserved it." Still, if her positive manner sometimes rubbed people the wrong way, Margaret Roberts also had more likable qualities. She always shared the chocolate that her father gave her when she went home for lunch.

Margaret was the daughter of a hardworking grocer

with very strict ideas about right and wrong. "You mustn't follow the crowd because you're afraid of being different," he warned her. "You decide what to do yourself and, if necessary, you lead the crowd."

Her father, Alfred Roberts, had been a tall and handsome boy with pale yellow hair. The son of a country shoemaker, he had wished that he could be a teacher. When he was thirteen, though, he had to quit school and start earning money.

Still, he set his mind on doing better than his own father had—and he went to town, where he got a job as a grocer's assistant. He worked so hard that, at twenty-one, he was promoted to be manager of the shop. In a few more years he had saved enough from his wages to buy a shop of his own.

Above it were several rooms where a family could live. Now he felt ready to marry, and he chose a young woman as serious-minded as he was. In fact, he had met Beatrice Stephenson at a Methodist prayer meeting.

She, too, came from a low-income background. Her father had been a railway guard and, since her girlhood, she had been helping her family by sewing clothing for rich ladies. After Beatrice married Alfred in 1917, they both worked harder than ever.

Their first child, a daughter they named Muriel, was born in 1921. By then they had expanded the grocery store to twice its former size, and it also contained a branch of the post office. In addition, Mr. Roberts had done a good deal of studying by himself, especially books about religion.

As a result, he began preaching sermons at Methodist chapels in the area. Instead of being known as just a storekeeper, he won added prestige because of his preaching.

Then Mr. Roberts went further. He started to take an active part in local politics, and he was elected to the town council. All on his own, without the slightest help from rich or powerful relatives, he became a respected man in the community.

Although the rooms above the shop were kept spotlessly clean by Mrs. Roberts, they lacked many comforts. Only cold water came from the faucet of the kitchen sink and, if warm water was wanted, a kettle had to be heated. In this far-from-grand home, Margaret Hilda Roberts was born on October 13, 1925.

The building Margaret lived in—of dreary, dark red brick—had no garden at all. It stood smack on the corner of two noisy roads, bustling with heavy traffic between London and the north. In the 1930s, though, when Margaret was going to school, many families would have been pleased to have a home like hers.

About twenty-five thousand people were living in Grantham then, and probably half of them had even fewer comforts. But the idea of fitting just somewhere near the middle of any group certainly did not appeal to the second daughter of Alfred Roberts. Right from the start Margaret showed a terrific ambition to be a leader.

At the age of five she began taking piano lessons. In just a few weeks she caught up with—and then passed—her older sister, Muriel. "Margaret was always about three lessons ahead of me," Muriel recalled many years later.

Although Margaret outdid Muriel in many ways, the sisters got along well together. For their parents did not allow any squabbling. "If you were rude or naughty you were sent to your room and you stayed there until you came down and apologized," Margaret herself recalled long afterward. "But this didn't seem to happen all that often."

Both girls were taught to help their mother, and Mrs. Roberts set them an example of never wasting a minute. When they came down for breakfast, sometimes she had already finished baking two or three pies—more than they needed themselves, so that she could give a little present to a sick neighbor. "She's a good woman," local people said about Margaret's mother.

Still, Margaret felt closer to her father. Because she seemed unusually bright, he got into the habit of talking to her about the events of the day as he would have talked to a son if he had had one.

Margaret even looked like her father. She had the same light-blue eyes and finely molded features, although her hair was brown. Actually, she might have been raised to think of herself as quite pretty—if she had been born into a family that put any importance on having a pretty face.

But the high-minded Mr. Roberts praised this daughter for being intelligent. And by the time she was ten, Margaret had found a special interest. That year, a heated election contest made many men stop in at the shop. While her father stood slicing bacon, he discussed politics with them. One evening Margaret was helping out by scooping sugar from the large bin into small packets. She listened eagerly to the men, and even dared to ask whether there was anything *she* could do for the cause.

So her father gave her a job. On the day of the election she stood outside the place where people were voting, feeling thrilled. From time to time she was handed a list of the names of those who had already cast their ballots. Then she ran like mad to deliver the list to the office of her father's political party. There the names were checked off, and other messengers hurried to remind party supporters who had not yet voted.

But it never occurred to Margaret that she might someday run in an election herself. For women had only recently been granted the right to vote. Politics still seemed to be a man's world. Young as she was, though, Margaret already had one definite goal.

She wanted to go to a university—and her father very much wanted her to have this opportunity, which he had missed. That meant she would soon have to pass a difficult exam. Only the most capable students were admitted to the upper, or grammar, school where pupils were prepared for a higher education.

Margaret was good at taking exams. Once, a severe thunderstorm had shaken the town while her class was taking a test. Another girl asked her later if she hadn't been terrified by the thunder claps. Margaret looked puzzled. She had been concentrating so hard on what she was writing that she hadn't heard a sound!

It was not too surprising, then, that Margaret did win a place in grammar school when she was just ten and a half—six months ahead of the usual age of eleven.

In grammar school Margaret ranked at the top of her class every year except one. She came out second then. Always neatly dressed and well-behaved, she made the mothers of some of her classmates ask their daughters an annoying question: "Why can't *you* be more like Margaret Roberts?"

Even so, Margaret herself sometimes wished that

she could be more like other girls. Because of the strict religious beliefs of her parents, she was not allowed to go to dances—and she had to attend several church meetings every week. That left her very little time for having fun.

As a special treat, sometimes she and Muriel were allowed to see a movie on a Saturday afternoon. Margaret particularly liked watching Ginger Rogers and Fred Astaire. Secretly she thought of becoming an actress.

But the Roberts girls were taught to be sensible about picking a career in which they would be sure to earn money. When Muriel was seventeen, she was sent away to study physical therapy, a type of nursing. Margaret was thirteen then, and she began thinking about becoming a chemist because her teacher said jobs for females were opening up in this field. During the next few years Margaret decided, too, that she wanted the best possible training. Rather than go to any ordinary university, she would go to Oxford!

The headmistress of Margaret's grammar school plainly disapproved when she heard what this daughter of a local grocer had in mind.

It wouldn't do, Miss Gillies said. A girl like Margaret had better not try to push herself beyond her proper place in life. Why not aim for the nearby University of Nottingham, instead?

Margaret shook her head.

Then Miss Gillies raised another question. Did Margaret know that Latin was required—five years of Latin—to pass the entrance exam at Oxford? Margaret had been taking plenty of chemistry, but no Latin at all.

If she needed Latin, Margaret replied, she would find someone to give her private lessons.

And she did. In just a year she crammed enough Latin into her head to pass the Oxford exam with a high mark. Still, she had to do more than merely gain admission. Because her father could not possibly afford what it cost to attend Oxford, Margaret also had to win a scholarship.

As it worked out, she won only a partial grant. But Mr. Roberts felt very proud of her and said he somehow would pay the rest. In the autumn of 1943, when Margaret was just about to turn seventeen, she left her home above the grocery shop—on her way to Oxford.

2

"Yes, I *Ought* to Be an M.P."

Margaret felt awfully homesick at first. As a chemistry student, she had to spend long hours doing lab experiments. Then, late every afternoon, she would make herself a lonely cup of tea in her own room. Soon, though, the magic of Oxford began to captivate her.

When she arrived there near the end of 1943, World War II was not yet won. With her family she had listened to mostly distressing news over the radio every evening since Britain entered the terrible conflict back in 1939. Still, life in the old town of Grantham had gone on almost as usual.

Oxford, though, was excitingly involved with great events. Because its beautiful stone buildings were a heart-stirring symbol of England's glorious past, the threat of enemy air raids worried everybody. So Margaret volunteered to serve as a fire watcher several hours a week. Thankfully, no enemy planes dropped any bombs, but the experience gave her a tremendous sense of patriotism. Until the war ended in 1945, Margaret also devoted one evening every week to working at a snack bar for soldiers stationed in the area.

Even before the marvelous news of the Allied victory, Oxford had kept right on with its 600-year-old tradition of training the nation's future leaders. Unfortunately, though, some narrow ideas had by no means been forgotten. Most of the students at Oxford were the sons of wealthy families with high social positions. Among the small number of women admitted, the majority belonged to the same privileged class.

So, as a grocer's daughter, Margaret might have felt quite uncomfortable. But she refused to let herself be fazed by snobbery. In fact, she refused even to think of herself as an outsider.

Hadn't her father's example taught her that hard work would be rewarded? What's more, she shared his political views about the importance of upholding

tried-and-true values—of supporting the Conservative party. As a result, Margaret began doing more than merely studying chemistry. She boldly joined the Oxford University Conservative Association.

OUCA, the students called it. Because many of Britain's political leaders had attended Oxford, OUCA often welcomed well-known guest speakers. And Miss Margaret Roberts soon demonstrated that she had the nerve to question them sharply.

"Does the speaker think . . . ?" Her queries on many different topics enlivened OUCA meetings. Some of her fellow students enjoyed her boldness. "Trust Margaret!" they said when she rose to ask a tough question, but others took a different attitude. "She's at it again!" they groaned.

Even so, during her third year at Oxford, Miss Margaret Roberts became the first woman ever to be chosen as OUCA's president.

It was not until a year later, though, that she openly admitted what she had begun thinking. After the twenty-first birthday party of a friend, Margaret stayed late with a group of clean-up helpers. In the kitchen a hot discussion started about the Labour party's recent election victory.

Margaret spoke up with such vigor that someone said to her, "Well, then, you'd really like to become a Member of Parliament?"

Margaret nodded decisively. "Yes," she said. "I *ought* to be an M.P."

Approaching her twenty-third birthday, Miss Margaret Roberts had completed her university training and was working for a plastics firm near the small city of Colchester. But her job of testing a new sort of glue interested her only mildly.

At the rooming house where Margaret lived, she impressed her landlady as a very well-dressed young woman. "Nice suits, nice blouses, nice gloves," Mrs. McAuley said approvingly.

Altogether, Margaret gave most people who knew her a favorable impression. She was five and a half feet tall, with an attractive figure—a bit on the plump side, but she kept her weight down by being extremely strict with herself about eating sweets. Also, she somehow managed that not a strand of her neatly permed hair was ever out of place. Especially when she smiled, she looked quite pretty.

But she felt she was wasting time. Then, in 1948, Margaret was chosen to represent Oxford graduates at the annual conference of the Conservative party. The Tories, as the Conservatives were often called, met in a seaside town.

During a lunch break she and a friend from Oxford went for a walk along the waterfront. They were joined by John Miller, the Conservative chairman of Dartford, not far from London.

Margaret's friend was an older man who ran a big bookstore. "I hear," he said to John Miller, "that you're trying to find a candidate to fight the next election."

"Oh, yes," Miller said. "We shall need a very able young man. It's a very tough industrial area."

Margaret's friend spoke up again. "Would you consider an able young woman?"

"Oh, no, it's not that sort of area at all."

"Well, would you just consider her?"

Miller shrugged. "She can apply," he said.

Of course, Margaret knew that an area like Dartford must be "safe" for the Labour party. Both Labour and her own Conservatives could count on winning certain districts in every Parliamentary election, because the people who lived in these districts almost always voted the same way.

But the British system allowed local political committees to select candidates who lived anywhere in the country. So it had become common for the two major parties to make good use of the other party's

safe districts. These served as tryouts for promising young candidates. If they did well in a few races where they could hardly be expected to win, sooner or later they would be chosen by a district where they would not have too much trouble getting elected.

Early in 1949 Margaret made a trip to Dartford to be interviewed by John Miller and his committee. She dressed with particular care, taking pains to look respectably stylish. More important, she had prepared a strong statement about her faith in the Conservative party.

Naturally, a district close to London was considered very desirable, even if winning it seemed unlikely, and twenty-three other hopeful candidates also appeared. At the end of a long day all but three had been politely rejected.

Miss Margaret Roberts was one of the trio asked to return a few weeks later. Then each of the three had to address a crowd of local voters. Anyone wishing to speak on their behalf also would be heard.

Margaret herself made a short talk in which she promised to work very hard for Dartford's interests. Then her father, recently chosen as mayor of Grantham, proudly spoke up for his daughter. When he sat down, the meeting surprised John Miller.

With only one dissenting vote, Margaret Roberts was selected. No matter that all the others who applied had been men. No matter that, at twenty-three, she would be the youngest woman candidate in the country. On February 28, 1949, she was formally "adopted" by Dartford.

But that same date had even more personal importance for Margaret. It was quite late when the meeting in Dartford ended. How could she get back to Colchester in time to go to work the next morning? A tall, friendly man at the meeting volunteered to drive her.

His name was Denis Thatcher.

Until recently he had been Major Denis Thatcher. When he put away his uniform, after six years in the Royal Artillery, he went to work for the business his grandfather had founded. His grandfather had noticed that a particular chemical protected sheep against various ailments. From this had come a profitable company dealing in agricultural chemicals.

Denis was much less serious-minded than Margaret. He loved games, especially golf and rugby. At the age of thirty-six, he delighted in driving fast in his Jaguar sports car.

Yet he fully shared Margaret's devotion to the Conservative party. And soon he made it clear that he felt very devoted to Margaret herself. Even if many of his ideas were old-fashioned, he told her he saw no reason why a talented young woman should give up her own career when she found a husband.

Margaret had thought she probably would not marry. But Denis did his best, during the next two years, to make her change her mind. He had no easy time, though.

For Margaret was determined to make a good showing in her political debut. It was January 1950 when a national election was finally called—and she began her campaign. By then she already was a familiar figure to Dartford's voters.

In order to spend as much time as possible going from house to house, she had rented a room in the town. But she still needed to support herself, so she had found a job in the research department of a chain of restaurants. All week long she took a train into the city at ten past seven in the morning, worked all day at testing new sorts of fillings for pastry, and caught a train back at ten past six. After a quick meal she set out to convince people who usually voted for the Labour party's candidate to vote for her instead.

These were mostly working people whose loyalty to the Labour cause was based on its support of programs like social security. Talking with them, Margaret used her father's favorite example—of a canary bird in a cage.

"It has social security," she said. "It has food and warmth and so on. But what is the good of all that if it has not the freedom to fly out and live its own life?"

Margaret's tireless efforts did make a difference.

Traditionally, Dartford had given the Labour candidate a majority of 20,000 votes. In 1950 that margin was cut by almost one-third, to only 13,000 votes.

As a result, Margaret was chosen to run again when another national election was called in September 1951. She had really been campaigning almost continuously, but she was not quite as single-minded as she seemed.

Soon after she lost the second election—shaving another 1,000 votes from the Labour total—several London papers printed smiling pictures of Miss Margaret Roberts. At the age of twenty-six, on December 13, 1951, she married Denis Thatcher.

3

Mrs. Thatcher Prepares

Margaret became Mrs. Thatcher at a simple ceremony—in a Methodist church in the old part of London. Since it was a cold, foggy day, she was glad she had decided against the usual sort of gown. Instead, she wore a warm blue velvet that would serve nicely as her best dress during the coming winter. More festively, her matching hat was trimmed with an enormous white ostrich feather.

A few months after her wedding, she and all of Britain were thrilled by a far grander ceremony. Even

if the country had long been a democracy, where the people elected their actual lawmakers, they were still extremely fond of their royal family. So it was quite a holiday, on June 2, 1953, when a twenty-five-year-old princess was crowned as Queen Elizabeth.

The new Mrs. Thatcher could not help being struck by the fact that she herself was just a few months older than the new Queen. To her, this seemed a wonderful sign. She sat down and wrote an article that was printed by the popular *Sunday Graphic*.

"Wake Up, Women!" it was headed.

Mrs. Thatcher started out: "Women can—and MUST—play a leading part in the creation of a glorious Elizabethan era." The notion that married women should give up their own careers was mistaken, she insisted. For a career and family life could certainly be combined.

Yet Mrs. Thatcher soon discovered that doing so was not easy. If a woman wanted to go in for politics in a serious way, it surely helped to have a wealthy husband. Without the comfortable income that Denis earned, Margaret could not have taken a major step right after she married.

She started to study law. While she still believed her training as a chemist might someday help her, she thought that law would help her more. So she quit trying to find ways of keeping ice cream foamy and devoted full time to her new endeavor.

Early in 1953 Mrs. Thatcher was looking forward to taking her final law exam. Then she discovered a reason that her plan might be delayed. As it turned out, there were two reasons.

In August 1953 she gave birth—to twins. Suddenly she had a tiny son and a daughter, too. Some of Mrs. Thatcher's friends joked that she was just proving, once more, how efficient she was. After all, most women would have taken much longer to produce little Mark and also Carol.

To Mrs. Thatcher herself, however, the arrival of her two babies brought a special challenge. Caring for them would be a very demanding task. And if she put off striving to pass her law final, she might never go back to it.

Denis urged her not to quit studying. He said he could afford to pay a baby nurse, and he agreed with Margaret that she had "something else to give" besides motherly love.

So it happened that, only four months after her twins were born, Mrs. Thatcher did pass her bar exam.

In the next six years she never lost sight of her goal. Mrs. Thatcher felt no doubt at all that she would finally become a Member of Parliament. Meanwhile, she enjoyed some pleasant hours as a wife and mother.

The Thatchers lived in a style much beyond what

she had ever known before. Their first home was on one of London's charming side streets; then they moved to a much larger house in a prosperous suburb. Besides a nursemaid for the children, they employed two other servants.

Even so, Mrs. Thatcher made a point of always fixing breakfast for the family herself. She liked to cook and to putter over household chores on weekends. While Denis cheerily dug in their garden, she was happy pasting up some fresh wallpaper in one of their five bedrooms.

Mrs. Thatcher was much less strict with her children than her own parents had been. Now that she had become a mother herself, it was as if she suddenly realized how deeply she had wished she could have gone to picnics or birthday parties in her childhood. So she made sure that Mark and Carol had plenty of the "fun and sparkle" she had missed.

Another sign of Mrs. Thatcher's new attitude toward her own past was a decision she made about religion. She gave up the Methodist faith, with its severely simple style of worship, in favor of the less rigid and more fashionable Church of England. By doing so, she put an increasing distance between herself and her parents.

Some of Mrs. Thatcher's friends thought she had come to dislike any reminder of her days above the grocery shop. Her mother died during this period,

and her father soon remarried. After that, she rarely visited Grantham. Nor did she see much of her sister, who was now the wife of a farmer.

Instead, the young Mrs. Thatcher kept extremely busy with her own family and career. In addition to her domestic duties, she had begun practicing law, specializing in tax matters. She thought the experience would surely be useful when she did return to politics.

She tried, a few times, to become a candidate again. In the middle of the 1950s, though, she faced a problem she could not solve. As the mother of two small children, she was told repeatedly, it was her duty to stay home and look after them.

Mrs. Thatcher kept reminding party officials that she was working already, as a lawyer. Every weekday morning she took a commuter train into London and did not return home till evening. If she was elected to Parliament, she said, probably she would have more time with her children. In any case, she had excellent household help.

No matter! The men on various party committees shook their heads. It wouldn't look right, they insisted. Most people just wouldn't vote for a woman who was the mother of two young children.

In 1959, when her twins were six years old, Mrs. Thatcher tried again.

The district of Finchley, only a few miles north of Parliament Square, was the home of mostly upper-middle-class people. Until recently it had seemed quite safe for the Conservatives. But now another party—the Liberals—was making a serious effort to capture it.

So the local Conservative leaders were looking for "a real live wire" to represent them in the House of Commons, the more important of the two branches of Parliament. For all practical purposes, this House was the country's law-making body, and its elected delegates held the honorary title of M.P., for Member of Parliament.

The Finchley committee, in its quest for a likely candidate, interviewed one man after another. None of them gave the electric feeling that here was a sure winner. Without much hope, the committee began to question a well-dressed woman in her early thirties.

How would she go about defeating a strong Liberal campaign?

"I will get myself across to the people," Margaret Thatcher said briskly. "I will let them know what Conservatism is—and I will lead the troops into battle."

The chairman of the Finchley Conservatives leaned forward and asked several more questions. He found the answers intelligent as well as exciting. When he went home that evening, he amazed his wife.

"You'll never guess what's happened," he said. "I think we are going to have a woman M.P."

And he was right.

4

Member of Parliament

On October 20, 1959—exactly a week after Mrs. Thatcher's thirty-fourth birthday—she took her seat for the first time as a Member of Parliament.

Her arrival there caused quite a flurry. In the ornate chamber where the House of Commons met, women were no longer a tremendous novelty. That year 25 women had been elected, along with 605 men. But, especially in the Conservative party, a young and attractive female stood out very noticeably.

So newspaper photographers kept snapping pictures of Mrs. Thatcher. She was invited by charity groups to make speeches at their meetings. And the leaders of her party cannily began to treat her like a future star.

Most M.P.s merely represented the districts that had elected them. They sat in the back rows of the green leather benches on both sides of the House. The front rows were reserved for the M.P.s who had been asked by their party to help direct the running of the government. During recent years it had become politically wise to give one or two women lesser places down front—and, clearly, Mrs. Thatcher was being considered for such an honor.

But she certainly did not count on getting ahead without any effort on her part. When she was asked to speak in a House debate about a new pension plan, she made good use of her training as a lawyer. Her talk was so crammed with facts and figures that a political writer told his readers: "She stunned the House with statistics."

It was more important, though, that one of the most powerful men in the Conservative party told another leading Tory: "This woman is a bit different. Quite exceptionally able. A first-class brain."

Yet Mrs. Thatcher by no means won everybody's approval. For she had the kind of sharp voice and stern manner, when she spoke up in House debates, that reminded many men of some particularly un-pleasant schoolteacher from their own past.

In addition, what she said sometimes irritated even members of her own party. To start with, her views had seemed about the same as most other Conservative M.P.s. Their main idea was that the government should do as little as possible to interfere with private business or to stop British citizens from doing as they pleased.

But there had been a big change since the end of World War II, when the Labour party had been voted into power. During the next few years it had put through a series of new programs like its national health insurance plan, which vastly expanded the role of the government in British life. At first the Conservatives had opposed these Labour changes. Gradually, though, Labour's social welfare system had become more or less accepted among Conservatives, except in the extreme right wing of the party.

Here, reducing the government's influence and cutting taxes were the main concerns. And it still seemed that going back to "the good old days" was the best policy. In the troubled 1960s Mrs. Thatcher moved further and further toward this right-wing point of view.

Even so, she received increasingly prominent positions in that wonderful British invention called the Shadow Cabinet. Since Labour was again running the country, the actual Cabinet was headed by the top man in the Labour party. Of course, Prime Minister Harold Wilson chose Labour M.P.s to direct every department of the government.

But the Conservatives "shadowed" Wilson and his aides—something like the way policemen shadowed suspects to make sure no crime would be committed. The leader of the Tories, as most people usually referred to the Conservatives, was a clever man named Edward Heath. He served as the Shadow Prime Minister. In 1969, when Margaret Thatcher was forty-four, he chose her to be his Shadow Secretary for Education.

A writer for the *Sunday Telegraph* asked Mrs. Thatcher if her appointment made her think that she might someday rise much higher. Did she dream of becoming the country's first woman Prime Minister?

Mrs. Thatcher fixed icy blue eyes on this foolish interviewer. "No woman in my time will be Prime Minister," she sharply lectured him.

A year later, in 1970, the Conservatives returned to power. Then Prime Minister Heath appointed Mrs. Thatcher as his real Secretary for Education. It was a very difficult job.

Student rebels had taken up all sorts of ideas that shocked their elders. Instead of "proper" clothing, they wore blue jeans. They shouted protests about the Vietnam War and about old ways of teaching, and strongly favored some of the Labour party's programs.

But the Conservatives had promised to reverse these Labour plans for modernizing the schools. Also, the Tories had pledged to cut government spending—and Mrs. Thatcher found herself having to defend a severe cut involving the nation's children. In the new budget no money at all was provided for free milk in the schools.

Suddenly, wherever Mrs. Thatcher went, there were angry shouts. "Thatcher, Thatcher, the milk snatcher!" people chanted. When she arrived to take part in a ceremony at a large school, the crowd outside was whipped into a frenzy by a furious young man. "Do you hate Mrs. Thatcher?" he hollered. "YES!" the crowd yelled.

Outwardly calm, Mrs. Thatcher carried on day after day. Only later did she admit that, sometimes when

she went home at night, she could not help shedding a few tears. One of those occasions must have come in November 1971.

Then, the *Sun* printed a long story about her, under the headline:

THE MOST UNPOPULAR WOMAN IN BRITAIN

By February 1974 Prime Minister Heath was so unpopular himself that he had to give the signal for a new national election. Voters who had become fed up with his failure to solve the country's economic problems then chose Labour again. This defeat started a year of surprising turmoil in the Tory party.

To understand what happened, it is necessary to keep in mind that the people of Britain do not elect their Prime Minister, except indirectly. They vote for individual members of Parliament, who belong to one or another of the country's political parties. Then, if the Tories win a majority of the seats in Parliament, the leader of the Tories becomes Prime Minister.

So the title of party leader is of great importance. Each party has its own method for choosing its leader. In 1974 a good deal of grumbling started among Conservative M.P.s because the Tory method no longer suited them.

Always in the past a Tory leader had kept his title— once he was chosen—until one of two things happened. Either he decided himself to resign or the decision was taken out of his hands if he was defeated in his own race for reelection to Parliament.

Since Edward Heath had managed to keep his seat, the second condition did not apply. Nor did he pay any attention when it was suggested by some Tory writers that he really ought to step aside. As a result, a revolt against his leadership began gathering steam.

Mrs. Thatcher was well aware that, without loyalty to the party leader, the British system would not work. Despite her anti-Heath opinions—she felt, for instance, that he was not nearly tough enough in dealing with unions—she took no open part in the growing campaign against him.

In June a reporter from the *Liverpool Post* challenged her to admit that she herself had a strong ambition. Yes, she said. She did hope that, sooner or later, she might rise to a position for which her experience as a tax lawyer had prepared her. What she wanted was nothing less than the second highest post in the country—the job of directing the country's finances as Chancellor of the Exchequer.

But how about becoming party leader? Then, if the Tories won the next election, she would take over the top job as Prime Minister.

Mrs. Thatcher frowned. "It will be years before a

woman either leads the party or becomes Prime Minister," she said. "I don't see it happening in my time."

Less than six months later she changed her mind. For not a single man had agreed to oppose Heath openly. One of the likely candidates insisted that private business reasons prevented him from making the move. Another said his wife would not be able to stand being in the public spotlight. But it was obvious that something else was holding the men back.

They did not dare to fight Heath. They were afraid that, if they lost the fight, their own political careers would be ruined.

Mrs. Thatcher faced the same risk. Still, she took the chance. During the next few months an intensely complicated struggle went on, mostly behind the scenes. As far as newspaper readers could tell, "Maggie" had no real hope of winning the party leadership. Surely she was just a stand-in. One man or another would take over the support that she was gaining—if Heath *was* forced to resign.

But a week after Heath did resign, there was a history-making vote. On February 11, 1975, in one of the committee rooms of the House of Commons, nearly three hundred Tory M.P.s cast their ballots for their party's next leader. By a clear majority of 53 percent, Margaret Thatcher won the title.

How did it happen?

The experts did their best to explain this astounding triumph by a woman. In effect, their answer was simply:

"She was the only one who had the guts to run."

5

At Last,
Prime Minister

At the age of forty-nine, Mrs. Thatcher had proved to the entire world that a woman could master the art of politics. Sometimes it suited her, though, to pretend that she was really just a housewife.

By now she and her husband had a comfortable home not far from Parliament Square. In its ground-floor kitchen she continued to fix breakfast for Denis almost every morning. Although he traveled a lot in connection with his business, and he also was the referee at many rugby matches, the Thatchers valued the time they spent together.

Mrs. Thatcher liked to say that Denis was her "shock absorber." She always felt soothed after talking over her troubles with him, she explained. Yet he himself stayed out of the public eye as much as possible.

As for their son and daughter—the twins were twenty-one when their mother became the Tory leader—they had grown up away from the excitement of politics. Mark and Carol had both attended boarding schools. Now Carol was thinking of studying law or trying to be a writer. Mark, who enjoyed life without having any special ambition, thought he might go into some business that would allow him plenty of time for fun.

But Mrs. Thatcher's startling victory gave the whole family a taste of fame. They all posed, with beaming smiles, in front of television cameras. Still, Denis and the twins refused to be interviewed.

Mrs. Thatcher herself took on the burden of being a public figure. As party leader, she now had the enormously challenging job of Shadow Prime Minister. It was up to her to direct the Tory opposition so skillfully that Labour would lose its narrow margin—and then she would take over as the actual Prime Minister.

Never before in British history, however, had a Shadow P.M. faced anything like Mrs. Thatcher's problem. She not only had to sweep away a great deal of prejudice against the mere idea of having a woman as the head of the government. She also had to change

some very unfavorable personal opinions that many people had formed about her.

Even among Tories, she was often referred to as "a cold fish." Some of her friends told reporters that, behind Mrs. Thatcher's outer stiffness, she was really a very warmhearted woman. They said she was quick to sympathize with their problems, and that she always chose extremely thoughtful presents for her assistants. Still, she could not seem to show the public any softer side of her nature.

Nor had she paid much attention to changing styles. So London's bright, young, trendy set made a lot of cutting remarks about Mrs. Thatcher. One writer dismissed her as incredibly boring and outdated—"A woman who sounds as though she is always wearing a hat."

But Mrs. Thatcher knew that the trendy set would be against her no matter how she looked or spoke. It was what she stood for that they really opposed— quite rightly, because bringing back "the good old days" could never appeal to them.

Although Mrs. Thatcher personally was very different from America's warm and likable President Reagan, their political ideas were similar. So she was popular among the rich and other solidly conservative voters. "She's got her head screwed on right," they said approvingly. But she needed much wider support for her party to win the next election.

And she felt sure she could restore Britain's prosperity and restore its leading position among the free nations if she could only reach some groups that usually voted for Labour. Just as one example, weren't the wives of many union members disgusted by all the bitter strikes that had been tearing the country apart? Why couldn't she make them understand that she truly had their best interests at heart?

"I am what I am, and I will stay that way," Mrs. Thatcher told them; then she added: "I just hope to improve in communicating."

Toward that end, she took lessons aimed at making the tone of her voice less sharp. She also had her hair tinted a flattering reddish blonde. And she sought advice from a smartly dressed Tory friend about new clothes to wear for television appearances.

All this may have helped to improve Mrs. Thatcher's image. Yet she did not soften her political opinions one bit. She kept repeating her right-wing ideas with such a deep sincerity that people who'd never dreamed of voting Tory started to wonder: Might Maggie really do the country some good?

Mrs. Thatcher realized, though, that her biggest difficulty involved foreign affairs. Somehow, she had to prove that a woman would be able to uphold Britain's interests in its dealings with other countries. So she took several trips around the world, speaking up wherever she went. What helped her most of all, though, was an angry outburst by a Russian official.

Mrs. Thatcher had made a speech at a London meeting, in which she said some harsh words about the Soviet Union. She accused it of being "bent on world dominance." This was during a period when America and its British ally were trying to reach an agreement with the Communists. Although Mrs. Thatcher had no real power then, the Russian reaction to her speech was very strong.

In Moscow a bitter protest was printed about the remarks by "the Iron Lady." That phrase made a Tory spokesman in London smile broadly. "It's worth a million votes to us," he said.

When a national election was called in the spring of 1979, Mrs. Thatcher started a whirlwind campaign all over Britain. Strictly speaking, she herself was running just for another term as the Member of Parliament from the London district of Finchley. Still, it was up to her to convince voters everywhere to choose a Tory M.P. because, if the Tories won a majority, *she* would become Prime Minister.

At a crowded rally in the city of Birmingham, Mrs. Thatcher was inspired to put aside the rather preachy speech she had planned to read. "The Russians said I was an Iron Lady," she briskly reminded her audience, and the words brought a burst of applause. "They were right!" Mrs. Thatcher shouted. That caused even louder cheering. Leaning forward, Mrs. Thatcher waited till she could be heard, and then she added: "Britain *needs* an Iron Lady."

Day and night, throughout the five-week campaign, Mrs. Thatcher tirelessly kept on promising to solve the country's problems. Toward the end her voice was nearly gone. Then her husband, who had been smilingly but silently accompanying her, gave the press a few words of his own.

When his wife paused on her way to board a plane, and began to greet some well-wishers waiting along her path, Denis firmly grasped her arm. "Walk, dear, don't talk," he said.

Mrs. Thatcher did accomplish the goal she had boldly set for herself. She not only won in Finchley by the biggest majority she had ever received. All over the country, the Conservatives won a safe margin of forty-three seats in the House of Commons.

So the day after the election, on May 4, 1979, Margaret Thatcher, at the age of fifty-three, became Great Britain's first woman Prime Minister.

And what did she achieve after she took over as the head of the government? Only in the future will it be possible for students of history to give a clear answer to this question. It is still too soon to know if Mrs. Thatcher will rank among Britain's outstanding Prime

Ministers—or if she will be remembered just because she was the first woman.

Certainly, she tried extremely hard to change the direction Britain had been taking. But her vigorous efforts brought very mixed results. On the plus side, she succeeded in stopping the terrible rise in prices that had been plaguing the country. Instead of inflation, though, her policies brought more unemployment.

Then another sort of crisis erupted in the Falkland Islands, some British territory thousands of miles away, off the coast of South America. Mrs. Thatcher's decisive leadership in the short war there raised her popularity so much that the Tories won another national election in 1983.

A year later she narrowly escaped death from a terrorist's bomb. It went off at three o'clock in the morning, wrecking part of a hotel where she was staying. If Mrs. Thatcher had been asleep then, she probably would have been killed. But she was still up, writing a speech—and she bravely delivered it, right on schedule, the next day.

So even her enemies granted her high marks for her personal courage. But she did have many enemies. Both personally and politically, Mrs. Thatcher made it easier for people to respect her than to like her.

At a gathering to promote the British fashion industry, she gave a good example of her prickly manner. A well-known dress designer was wearing a T-shirt protesting one of Mrs. Thatcher's policies. The shirt said: "58% Don't Want Pershing," which meant that a majority in the country didn't want American missiles stationed there.

Instead of making a joke of the designer's daring, Mrs. Thatcher smiled frostily as she read the message. "We can't always have what we want," she instructed the woman. "Sometimes we have to have what's good for us."

Also, her lack of any sense of humor distressed many Britons. Once, in the House of Commons, Mrs. Thatcher jumped up during a debate about taxes and announced, "I have the latest red-hot figure!" The peals of laughter that rang out completely baffled her.

Later Mrs. Thatcher explained to a reporter that she really didn't think in terms of being a woman. She thought of herself as a politician who happened to have been born female. She saw no reason for the govenment to give women special help—just as she was against giving special help to any group.

Mrs. Thatcher herself put it this way: "If somebody comes to me and asks, 'What are you going to do for small businessmen?' I say, 'The only thing I'm going to do for you is make you feel freer to do things for yourselves. If you can't do it *then,* I'm sorry, I'll have nothing to offer you.'"

Still, Mrs. Thatcher's ways of making people "feel

freer" caused a great deal of controversy. Her tough policies toward unions, her changes in the tax laws, her efforts to limit expensive welfare programs—all these brought a lot of dispute.

According to her supporters, Mrs. Thatcher was like a doctor who had to use strong medicine to cure her patient. Those who opposed her, though, claimed that she was really helping only the rich.

On just one question hardly anybody disagreed with Mrs. Thatcher. Whether they liked her or not, they said that she did have an exceptional talent for politics.

She herself had made this point back in 1975. Right after she won the post of party leader, she had held a news conference.

"Why do you think you won?" a reporter asked her.

"Merit," said Mrs. Thatcher crisply.

ABOUT THIS BOOK

I wish I could have met Mrs. Thatcher. While I was in London, reading about her in back issues of British newspapers, I telephoned her office to see if an appointment was possible. No, she was much too busy. And members of her family did not talk with writers, I was told.

So I watched her on television. I went to Grantham and saw her birthplace and the red brick school she attended as a girl. Then I was able to take advantage of the day-by-day experience of some reporters I knew from my own days of working for *The New York Times*. Thanks to them, I felt almost as if I, too, had watched Mrs. Thatcher's rise to Prime Minister.

For any readers who would like to find out what Mrs. Thatcher has been doing since 1984, when this book was written, I suggest a visit to your public library. Leading American newsmagazines often cover British politics. Ask the librarian to help you look up "Thatcher, Margaret"—and that should bring you up to date. Good luck!   D.F.